Building a
community
of readers

Book-Rich
Environments
Initiative

ACPL

Fort Wayne
Urban League

Project
READS

fwha
FORT WAYNE housing authority

a house that once was

Written by *Julie Fogliano* Illustrated by *Lane Smith*

ROARING BROOK PRESS • NEW YORK

Deep in the woods
is a house
just a house
that once was
but now isn't
a home.

At the top of a hill
sits the house
that is leaning.
A house that once wasn't
but now it is peeling.
A house that was once
painted blue.

Tiptoe creep
up the path
up the path that is hiding.
A path that once welcomed.
A path that is winding.
A path that's now covered in weeds.

At the front of the house
the house that is waiting
there's a door that is not really open
but barely.
A door that is closed
but not quite.
A door that is stuck between coming and going.
A door that was once painted white.

Off to the side there's a window
that's watching.
A window that once opened wide.
A window that now has no window at all.
A window that says climb inside.

Inside the house
it is silent but creaking.
We're whispering mostly
but not really speaking.
We whisper though no one would mind if we didn't.
The someone who once was
is someone who isn't.
The someone who once was
is gone.

Who was this someone
who ate beans for dinner
who sat by this fire
who looked in this mirror?
Who was this someone
whose books have been waiting
whose bed is still made
whose pictures are fading?

Who was this someone
who walked down this hallway
who cooked in this kitchen
who napped in this chair?
Who was this someone
who left without packing
someone who's gone
but is still everywhere?

Was it a man with a big beard and glasses

who would look out the window and dream of the sea?

Or a woman who painted all day in the garden

portraits of squirrels while sipping iced tea?

Was there a cat who would sleep by the fire

or a girl who would twirl to her records and sing?

A boy who built planes and dreamt nightly of flying?
A baby? A cowboy? A queen or a king?

Why did they leave here and where were they going?
Did they run off and not say goodbye?

Were they shipwrecked and now
live on an island
wearing coconut clothes with a pineapple tie?

Or maybe they took off and headed to Paris
where they paint by the river and eat lots of cheese.

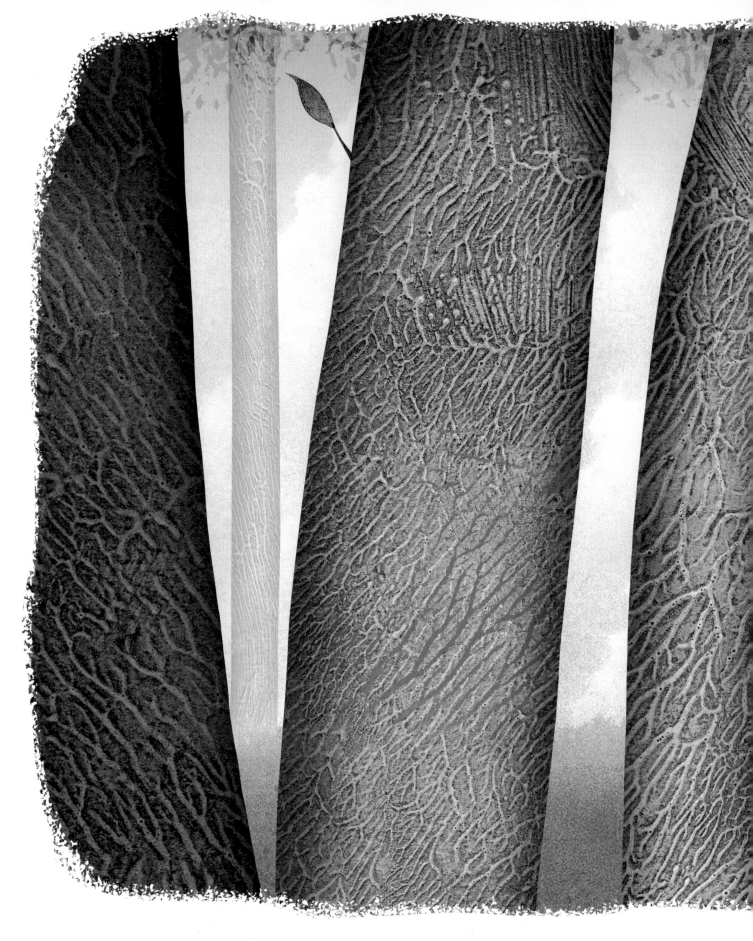

Or what if they're lost and they're wandering lonely?

Maybe they can't find their set of house keys?

And maybe the house is still waiting there for them. Waiting to hear their key turn in the door.

Waiting for voices to bounce down the hallway.
Waiting for someone to come sweep the floor.

Or maybe it loves to just sit and remember
stories of someone who we'll never know.
And maybe it likes it out there in the forest
with the trees coming in where the roof used to go.

So back through the window
we climb as we wonder.
Back down the path that is tangled with thorns.

Back to a house where our dinner is waiting.
Back to a home that is cozy and warm.

Deep in the woods
is a house
just a house
that once was
but now isn't
a home.

for the boys
who found a house
and wondered

and for lane
who knew just what to do
with wondering
—j.f.

For John and Malain
—L.S.

Text copyright © 2018 by Julie Fogliano
Illustrations copyright © 2018 by Lane Smith
Published by Roaring Brook Press
Roaring Brook Press is a division of Holtzbrinck Publishing Holdings Limited Partnership
175 Fifth Avenue, New York, NY 10010
mackids.com

Library of Congress Control Number: 2017955705

ISBN 978-1-62672-314-6

Our books may be purchased in bulk for promotional, educational, or business use. Please contact your local bookseller or the Macmillan Corporate and Premium Sales Department at (800) 221-7945 ext. 5442 or by e-mail at MacmillanSpecialMarkets@macmillan.com.

The illustrations in this book were done in two different techniques. The "present day" illustrations were made with India ink, drawn on vellum with a crow quill pen, then pressed while wet onto watercolor paper creating a blotted line effect. The colors were painted in oil over gesso then scanned and added digitally under the ink-line. The "imagined" scenes were painted in oil paint on hot press board and scanned along with paper collage elements that were combined digitally.

First edition, 2018
Book design by Molly Leach
Printed in China by RR Donnelley Asia Printing Solutions Ltd., Dongguan City, Guangdong Province

10 9 8 7 6 5 4 3 2